Fairy Tales
from Viet Nam

FAIRY TALES

FROM VIET NAM

Retold by Dorothy Lewis Robertson

ILLUSTRATED BY W. T. MARS

DODD, MEAD & COMPANY · NEW YORK

*To my three boys in the Nguyen family,
Luu, Thuan, and Kiem*

Author's Foreword

Collectors always take great pleasure in telling how they happened to find their little treasures. This is true whether the object is a sea shell, a rare coin, or a story. Just as a colored photograph reminds the traveler of a particularly pleasant moment in his trip, so does each item in a collection remind the collector of a moment of discovery.

The stories in this book have not been found in ancient manuscripts in a library, nor have they been recorded on tape by village elders. Instead they have been sent in letters from a war refugee in Saigon to his foster mother in the United States, sometimes in as many as four installments lasting over many months. The child is Nguyen Dinh Thuan, who, with his mother, grandmother, and two brothers, came from Haiphong in North Viet Nam when the division between north and south was made in 1954. After relocating in Saigon the mother found employment as a mat seller at eighty cents a day, and the three boys settled down in school.

Like all boys who have been studying hard for several months, the Nguyens look forward to any special event for diversion. In

October when our children are carving pumpkins into lanterns for Halloween, the Nguyens are working with bamboo and translucent paper making far more elaborate lanterns for the Lantern Procession in the Mid-Autumn or Children's Festival. Only Kiem will be in the procession this year as the older boys, Thuan and Luu, have grown up and are in secondary school. But they will watch, for they are pleased with the lantern that Kiem will carry.

While the boys are gone the mother sets out plates of melon seeds and moon cakes made from rice flour as a special treat for them when they return. Grandmother sits in the doorway of the one-room house and wonders which story she will be asked to tell tonight. Always after the Lantern Procession and before the boys go to bed, she tells them a story. It will be Kiem's choice tonight as he is the only young child left in the family. Soon he too will be grown-up like his brothers and much more interested in reading books than in hearing her stories.

Sitting there, the old lady thinks of all the stories she has told the boy and his two elder brothers—stories that went far back in history, how far back nobody knew. Generations of grandmothers had told them to their grandchildren and they in turn to their grandchildren. Some stories told about the lives of former emperors and their efforts to keep Viet Nam free. Some taught lessons in good conduct and others were told just for fun. All in some way reflected the beliefs of the Vietnamese people, and reminded them of their two-thousand-year struggle for independence. All provided a momentary escape from the harsh world of endless work and indebtedness into a dream world of wealthy mandarins, beautiful princesses, talking animals, dragons, and fairies.

The collection of stories in this book represents some of these very old tales, one of them going back to two hundred years before Christ. Rich in history and the religious beliefs of the people, they provide some insight into the character of the Vietnamese, and help to explain why they are willing to endure so much in order to be free. For two thousand years the fight against invaders and the revolt against the rule of foreign powers has been going on. Their first resistance was against the Chinese in 208 B.C., and again during the Ming Dynasty in A.D. 1408. Even during their brief period of freedom from the Chinese, between A.D. 939 and A.D. 1408, they were fighting off the Mongols under Kublai Khan in the north, the Khmers to the west, and the Chams in the south. From the time the Chinese General Trieu Da defeated the Emperor An Duong Vuong in 208 B.C. and incorporated the ancient kingdom of Au Lac, as Viet Nam was then called, into the province of Southeast China and proclaimed himself king, the Vietnamese have been striving continually to unify themselves as a nation and govern themselves under their own laws and the leadership of their own people. Today the struggle still goes on.

In this collection, the story of "The Emperor's Magic Bow" is one of the legends that is told about the Emperor An Duong Vuong, explaining how his defeat was caused by the treachery of his own daughter. The setting for the story is Co Loa which was the seat of government in ancient Au Lac and became the capital of Viet Nam when it finally won its freedom from Chinese rule under Ngo Quyen in A.D. 939.

During the thousand years of Chinese rule the Vietnamese dealt with Chinese administrators, merchants, and scholars, and since Viet

Nam was on the direct trade route between India and China, travelers
between these two countries stopped off there. As a result, the phi-
losophies and religions of both countries were introduced, blended,
and superimposed on the native religions of ancestor worship and
animism. Except for the Catholic minority, the Vietnamese even
today find nothing incongruous in combining Buddhism, Taoism,
and Confucianism, and at the same time are most particular to start
off their New Year's celebration, Tet, with offerings of rice to the
spirits of their departed ancestors who return home each year for
this occasion.

Through the teachings of Confucius each individual had a strict
code of behavior spelling out for him his duty to the family, especially the elder head of the family, and to the authorities in his village and province. The importance of honor and duty is seen in the
story, "The Three Who Couldn't Be Parted," in which the central
figure is a man who leaves his home for self-imposed exile when he
feels that he has dishonored the family. In "The Princess of Mount
Nam-Nhu," the mandarin's son has to renounce his title when he de-
cides to leave his family in order to search for the beautiful stranger
with whom he has fallen in love. In all of the stories, good behavior is
stressed and bad behavior is punished. Deceit, treachery, and greed
are dealt with firmly, and in "The Magic Ruby," a hunter who breaks
his promise to a raven winds up in jail.

The teachings of Buddha, with the emphasis on renouncing the
passions, desires, and problems of this life for the contemplation of
spiritual matters, were often in conflict with the teachings of Confucius. In Confucianism one could hope to get through this life by
abiding by the rules; in Buddhism the idea was to withdraw from

this life and through contemplation so purify one's soul that it could enter into the state of eternal happiness, Nirvana, instead of having to be reborn again. In the old days there was considerable dissension between the Confucists and the Buddhists, but over the years the two became assimilated and combined with the native religion of ancestor worship. The influence of Buddhism is seen in these stories in a mood of pessimism at times and the apparent willingness of people to commit suicide. Some people feel that this gives the stories a somber tone. Although this may be true in some of them, they still reflect the true nature of the Vietnamese, who lead, for the most part, a very somber life. Their history is so replete with generals and politicians who commit suicide when defeated that suicide itself cannot have the same overtones of immorality that it does for the Christians of the West.

As in all folklore of primitive peoples these old Vietnamese tales are full of animals that talk, idols that appear in different forms, and spirits of the mountains and sea. In the old days people believed that all things—animals, plants, rocks, and rivers—had spirits and personalities like humans, only more powerful. It is not surprising then, to find that the explanation of the occurrence each year of very heavy rains, the monsoon, revolves around the rivalry between Thuy Tinh, Lord of the Sea, and Son Tinh, Lord of the Mountain, to marry Emperor Hung Vuong's beautiful daughter.

In addition to such supernatural creatures, Vietnamese folklore also created a fascinating world of fairies who lived on a beautiful mountain that floated over the sea. The legend of the beginnings of Viet Nam goes back to the origin of these fairies. A beautiful woman, Au Co, married a handsome man, Lac Long Quam, and in the course of time produced one hundred children, fifty boys and fifty girls. The fifty girls went up to the mountains with their mother and became fairies and the oldest boy became the king of the country which he called Au Lac, a combination of the last names of his parents. The rest of the boys went down to the sea with their father to become dragons. The story, "The Princess of Mount Nam-Nhu," is laid partly in fairyland and tells of the adventures a mandarin's son has when he accidentally gets there while exploring a deep cave in a mountain.

The children who hear these stories told today are less interested in their historic or literary significance than they are in the feeling of wonder and fun that they evoke. Like boys and girls around the world, they want to hear the how's and why's of things explained in a fantastic sort of way. In spite of the scientific know-how of the average small child of today and the daily news reports of moon shots and orbiting in space, the youngsters in story hours are still enchanted by the tale, "Chu Cuoi's Trip to the Moon," and invariably bring back reports after the next full moon that they saw Chu Cuoi in his conical hat sitting at the foot of the banyan tree wondering how to get back to earth. Children's imaginations make no difference between East and West, and so with Kiem they delight in hearing these stories told again and again.

From grandmother to child the tales have come down for generations and, fortunately for us, in the Nguyen family one member was learning English. Elder brother Thuan welcomed a chance to practice his new language and at the same time earn a little money by setting down some of these stories in beginner's English. To realize what a tremendous task this was for him one would merely have to make the same proposition to an American high school student who was learning beginning French and watch the reaction. From Thuan's version of the stories to the present book meant some rewriting so that our boys and girls would find the tales readable. The author has also drawn on material from the letters written to her by Kiem over a period of six years to fill in some of the details, but has always tried to stay as close to Thuan's stories as possible. And that is how this book came to be written.

Contents

A Story for Kiem

In the autumn when the air is clear and cool and the moon is full and American children are carving pumpkins into lanterns for Halloween, the Vietnamese children are working with rice paper and bamboo, making their lanterns for the annual Children's Festival and Lantern Parade. This year the older brothers in the Nguyen family, Luu and Thuan, are in high school and are too old to be in the parade, so the honor of representing the family falls on the youngest brother, Kiem, who is only ten years old.

For days he and his elder brother, Thuan, have been cutting silhouettes of animals from rice paper, hanging them by threads from a little parasol which is raised inside the lantern over the candle. The heat from the lighted candle makes the parasol turn, and the animals, dangling on their threads, revolve like animals in a merry-go-round.

Kiem is very proud of his lantern. The other children may have bigger lanterns or brighter lanterns or ones shaped like fish or animals or stars, but he will have a lantern with pictures that move. Kiem holds it carefully by its bamboo frame so that it will not catch fire from the lighted candle inside. This year he hopes to carry his lantern to the very end of the parade and not have it burn up halfway through as it did last year.

It is a perfect night for the festival. The full moon shines brightly in a clear sky and makes the leaves on the trees glisten as though they are wet from a heavy rain. The air is cool and still and the lighted candles burn steadily in their lanterns. Kiem joins the procession that is moving slowly through the streets of Saigon, and Luu and Thuan join the older boys and girls who line the sides of the streets. It is fun to see the gay lanterns bobbing in the darkness, to hear the soft voices of the children singing as they march along.

Occasionally there is an anguished cry as some child carelessly swings his lantern and the thin rice paper bursts into flames and has to be quickly stamped out. Kiem is pleased

that this year his lantern is still burning brightly when the procession comes to an end and the other children gather round to admire his moving pictures.

After the parade is over, Kiem returns to his home and hangs his lantern on a post outside the family's one-room, thatched-roof cottage. His mother and grandmother have set plates of melon seeds and moon cakes made from fragrant rice flour on the table as a special treat for him. Kiem takes his to the doorway of the cottage and sits there with his grandmother, watching a tiny cloud drift across the face of the moon. It is a good night for moon watching. The shadows on the moon are especially clear and in Kiem's imagination they appear to be a banyan tree with spreading branches above and a little man in a cone-shaped hat sitting on one of the roots.

Always after the Lantern Procession his grandmother tells him a story and tonight Kiem asks for one of his favorites. "Ba Noi," he says, "tell me the story of the people with the long noses."

"That's a silly story," exclaims Luu, who comes through the front gate in time to hear the request. "What do you want to hear that one for? Who ever heard of people with noses like elephant trunks?"

"It was just punishment for wrongdoing," replies the grandmother. "See that the same doesn't happen to you."

Luu smiles good-naturedly at the reproof and sits down cross-legged on the hard-packed earth near the doorway. He still enjoys the stories his grandmother tells, even though he is much too old to believe them. "I like stories about real people," he says, "like the ones about the Emperor An Duong

Vuong and how he tried to keep the Chinese from conquering us."

"Yes, he tried," replies grandmother. "A long time ago that was, long, long ago—over two thousand years."

Kiem helps himself to another moon cake and says, "I wish I'd lived in those days. I'd have been a mandarin with a fine house and servants and a white horse to ride on."

Luu laughs at his younger brother's daydreams and teases him with, "You'd have been a peasant with a water buffalo to walk behind as you plowed a rice field. Be thankful you live today and can go to school."

Just then Thuan opens the gate and joins the others in the tiny yard. He squats beside Luu and cracks open a handful of melon seeds to eat. A little breeze rustles palm leaves on the thatched roof. Kiem leans his head against his grandmother's shoulder and yawns. It is way past his bedtime and he is beginning to feel sleepy, but he doesn't want to miss the story his grandmother will finally get around to telling. Grandmother puts her arm around him and says, "I know how you feel, Kiem. We all like to forget these troubled times. We have had no peace for over twenty years, so we like to think back on the days when Viet Nam was free and independent, with her own rulers, not the Chinese or French. And we like to tell stories about the people who fought for our freedom, stories of the Emperors An Duong Vuong and Ngo Quyen."

"I like stories that take you really far away," joins in Thuan, "not just back to the days of Emperors and mandarins. When I was your age, Kiem, I used to imagine I was walking across the clouds to fairyland the way Tu Thuc did. Only if I'd found a beautiful princess to marry I'd have stayed in fairyland forever."

"One look at you, Thuan, and the fairies would have pushed you through the clouds and you'd have fallen plop into the sea," laughs Luu.

"You boys are wasting time talking and Kiem hasn't had his story," grandmother says. "See, the moon is high in the sky and soon it will be time to go to bed."

The boys turn and look at the moon, full and round and silvery white.

"Can you see Chu Cuoi sitting at the foot of the banyan tree?" grandmother continues. "Did you boys know that we Vietnamese had a man on the moon long before the Russians and Americans even thought of it?"

She chuckles as the brothers look at her in surprise.

"No? Well, it happened this way...." And she begins to tell them the old, old story of "Chu Cuoi's Trip to the Moon."

Chu Cuoi's Trip to the Moon

Long, long ago there lived a poor woodsman named Chu Cuoi. Every day he went into the forest looking for logs to chop into firewood. These he tied together into bundles, then hung them on his long carrying pole and took them up to the village market to sell. He was so happy working in the forest that he never thought of taking a holiday, and on feast days when the market was closed and there was no one around to buy his wood, he was very sad.

So it happened that when the Festival of Tet came round and all the people were celebrating the New Year by shooting off firecrackers and settting bowls of rice on their household altars to welcome the spirits of their ancestors and dressing in new clothes to go calling on friends and relatives, Chu Cuoi was very downcast. He was too poor to buy any new clothes and the sputter and crackle of the firecrackers hurt his ears. With the market place closed for three whole days there would be no need for him to cut more firewood, and the idea of having nothing to do for such a long time made him restless. Why not celebrate the holiday in his own way, he thought, by following a path through the trees that he had seen many times but had never had a chance to explore?

It was very cool and quiet in the forest and Chu Cuoi was so busy listening to the birds and watching the butterflies he soon forgot to be sad. Suddenly he heard a strange sound ahead of him. Carefully he pushed aside a tangle of vines that had grown over the path and there on the other side of a little clearing were four tiger cubs tumbling about in front of a cave, snarling and growling as they played together. They pounced on each other and rolled over in the grass, biting and scratching with their teeth and claws, for all the world like four big kittens.

"If only I could capture them," said Chu Cuoi to himself, "I could sell their skins for a hundred piasters and buy myself a new suit, maybe even a new hat."

So he cut some lengths of tough vine and one by one caught

the little tigers and tied the four feet of each one together so that he could hang them on his carrying pole and take them home to skin them. Just as he was finishing he heard a loud growl behind him. It was the mother tiger coming home with a deer she had killed for dinner. Quietly Chu Cuoi slipped away from the cave and quickly climbed to the top of the nearest tree before the mother tiger could see him.

By this time the baby tigers were whining and whimpering because the tough vines around their legs were cutting into them. When the mother tiger saw what had happened, she let out a great roar and with her sharp teeth bit through the vines and set the cubs free. Then she licked their wounds to stop the bleeding, but when she saw how badly they were hurt she ran into the woods and soon came back with a mouthful of green leaves. These she chewed into little pieces and placed on the legs of her babies and in a few seconds, a few seconds only, the four little tigers were up and tumbling about as good as ever.

From his place high in the tree Chu Cuoi could see all this and wondered what magic leaves the mother tiger had used that would heal cuts and bruises so quickly. He thought if he could find the tree that they came from he would be able to

get some too. So the next day he walked down the path to
the clearing where he had seen the baby tigers playing. The
four of them were romping about just as they had been the
day before and the mother tiger was nowhere to be seen.
Again Chu Cuoi tied their legs together and then climbed up
into a tree to wait for the mother's return. Only this time
when she ran into the forest for the leaves, Chu Cuoi followed
at a safe distance until she stopped in front of a small tree that
was growing all by itself. She quickly bit off some of the
leaves and hurried back to her babies.

As soon as she was well out of the way Chu Cuoi carefully dug up the tree and carried it to his cottage by the edge of the forest where he planted it right in the middle of the garden. It didn't matter to him that he had to dig up some flowers to make way for the tree, or that as the tree grew, its roots spread far out across the garden and the flowers around it began to wither and die. Anyone could have a flower garden but only he had a tree whose leaves had the magic power to cure cuts in a matter of seconds. As it grew it looked more and more like a banyan tree, but Chu Cuoi felt sure there was no other tree in all the world like it.

So busy had Chu Cuoi been, taking care of his tree, that he hadn't been to the market place since the Festival of Tet. And since he hadn't been to market he hadn't heard any of the latest news. On this day tongues were wagging furiously. Much had been happening in the province and most important was the news that the Emperor's daughter was deathly ill with a strange disease. At the palace the court physicians and doctors from foreign lands had tried every medicine they knew, but nothing had helped her. The Emperor was beside himself with worry and as she grew weaker day by day he had a proclamation posted on the palace gate saying that to any-

one who could cure his daughter he would give half his kingdom and the princess's hand in marriage.

On the day that Chu Cuoi finally went up to market with
his load of firewood to sell, the princess had sunk into a deep
sleep and everyone feared that she would soon be dead. As
soon as Chu Cuoi read the proclamation he thought of his
magic leaves and, hoping to earn the rich reward and the
hand of the princess, he ran as fast as he could to gather a
handful of leaves from his tree and take them to the princess.

By the time he returned to the palace and had talked his
way past the guards and stood before the Emperor, he was
very hot and very dirty and in his old clothes with bits of bark
clinging to his hair, he hardly looked like a person who could
cure a mysterious disease. So when he asked to be allowed to
treat the princess with his leaves, the Emperor thought he was
being impudent and ordered his guards to beat him. The more
Chu Cuoi tried to explain about his leaves the harder the
guards beat him with bamboo canes until finally he fell un-
conscious on the floor.

How long he lay there he did not know, but when at last
he opened his eyes the sun was beginning to set outside the
palace window. Slowly he sat up and rubbed his shoulders

and arms. His back ached and his head swam and he was
covered with cuts and bruises. Near him stood one of the
Emperor's guards.

"Well now, beggar," he said. "If you are such a good doc-
tor, cure yourself."

Without a word Chu Cuoi picked up some of the leaves
that had fallen on the floor and put them in his mouth and

chewed them up and swallowed them. Immediately his cuts and bruises healed and he was able to stand on his feet just as strong as ever. The guard looked on in amazement and then hurried to tell the Emperor about the miracle. Before Chu Cuoi could leave the palace the Emperor himself came hurrying after him, full of apologies and pleading with him to try his cure on the princess.

He led Chu Cuoi to the princess's room where she lay, scarcely breathing. Her heart beat so slowly that each beat seemed to be the last and her rosy lips were almost blue. Chu Cuoi tore the last of his leaves into tiny pieces and gently pressed them into the princess's mouth. Gradually her heart beat faster, her breath became deeper, and soon the color came back into her lips and her eyes began to open. As though she were just waking from a deep sleep she looked up and smiled at Chu Cuoi.

The Emperor rejoiced to see his daughter restored to health and promptly gave Chu Cuoi half his kingdom as his reward. With some of his wealth Chu Cuoi built a beautiful castle where his cottage had once stood, and in the courtyard he kept his magic tree. As soon as everything was finished he brought his princess to live in her new home and for some time all went well with them. Chu Cuoi had a beautiful wife, a large fortune, and all the time he wished to wander in his beloved woods. But the princess was unhappy so far away from her home and, above all, she missed her flower garden.

One day she asked her husband if she could have some of the land in the courtyard for a flower garden. He readily agreed but warned her not to plant anything near the magic tree, for it would wither and die. The more the princess looked at the courtyard the more she wanted to have some bright flowers right in the center, in the very place where the magic tree stood. So one day while Chu Cuoi was out walking in the woods she started to dig a little around the tree to make a place for some flowers. Without meaning to, she cut one of the roots of the tree and a strange thing happened. The tree began to pull up out of the ground. Inch by inch each root began to work its way out of the dirt until at last only one long root held it to the ground.

Just at that moment Chu Cuoi returned and, with a loud cry, ran to the tree and caught hold of the root. He pulled as hard as he could to hold the tree to the earth, but with a sudden jerk the last root broke away and tree and root and Chu Cuoi went flying straight up to the sky. Chu Cuoi didn't

dare let go, so he just went up and up until finally he and the tree landed on the moon.

And now, on a clear night, they say, when the moon is full, you can see Chu Cuoi sitting on the root of the banyan tree, looking down at the earth and wondering how he will ever get back to his beautiful princess.

A Flower to Catch
a Thief

Long ago, when men and animals spoke the same language, a young man was told to take his master's water buffalo to a nearby field to graze. Although it was early in the morning, it was already very hot and mist rose from the field like steam. After he had turned the water buffalo loose in the field, the young man looked for a cool, shady place to wait until it was time to take the buffalo home. He found a spreading banyan tree near the edge of the field and so, having nothing better to do, lay down in its shade and went to sleep.

How long he slept he did not know, but when he awoke, the buffalo was nowhere to be seen. He looked everywhere for it, from one end of the field to the other, but not a trace could he find, not even a hoofprint. Thinking perhaps the

animal had started home alone, the young man followed the path back until he could see his master's house, but still there was no sign of the buffalo anywhere.

A great fear swept over the young man. How could he tell his master that he had let the buffalo get away? What punishment would the master give him? The thoughts of what might happen to him made him tremble and shake and he fell down to the ground and lay as though dead.

Just then an ugly, black crow flew down and started to settle on his face to pick out his eyes, but the young man quickly caught the crow by his legs and said, "You thought

I was dead, but I'm not and now I am going to wring your neck."

"Forgive me," said the crow. "You lay so still I thought you were dead. I don't wonder you want to kill me, but if you give me my freedom, I will give you something in return."

"What is it?" asked the young man, still holding on to the crow.

With that the crow opened his beak wide and out dropped a small piece of jade carved like a lotus blossom. "This is a magic jade," said the crow. "Hold this stone in your hand and all your wishes will become true."

The young man let the crow fly away and began to think of what to wish for. His first thought was of the missing water buffalo, so he said, "How happy I would be if I could have a buffalo to take to my master. It would make up for the one I lost." The words were hardly out of his mouth when he saw standing in front of him a fine, big buffalo. He quickly fastened a rope around his neck and led him to a shed and tied him to a post for the night.

From then on, every night after his master and his family had gone to sleep, the young man sat with the jade in his hand and tried wishing for things. It was just as the crow had said. The minute he wished for something, it was there in

front of him. A bowl of rice, a new coat, a bag of gold—
every wish was granted. Soon he was able to leave his master
and moved to a neighboring village where he bought a fine
house and lands of his own and in time became the richest
farmer in the countryside.

One evening he was sitting in his doorway, fondling the
jade and admiring the colors in the sky as the sun set behind
his fields, and the thought crossed his mind that it was very
lonely having no one sharing his new home with him. What
a pleasure it would be, he thought, to have a pretty, young
girl sitting next to him in the doorway, enjoying the sunset
with him. How he wished he could share his good fortune
with a wife.

Just at that moment he looked down the road that led to
his home and there he saw walking toward him a beautiful
young girl, the daughter of one of the richest farmers in a
nearby village. From her cone-shaped straw hat to the sandals
on her bare feet, she was everything he could have wished for.
A sudden gust of wind blew off her hat and rolled it right up
to the doorway where it came to rest at the young man's feet.
Naturally, the two young people felt that this was a good
omen and that a kind fate meant them for each other. So the
two were married and the young man thought he could never

be happier. All went well with them until one day the wife asked him how he became so wealthy.

"Isn't it true that a short time ago you were a servant?" she said. "How have you become rich so quickly?"

The foolish man told her the story about the crow and showed her the beautiful jade piece which he had only to rub to have his wishes granted. Then he started off to the market to sell his rice. While he was gone the wife stole the jade and ran back home to her family.

When the young man returned from market and found

that not only was his wife gone but that she had taken his magic jade with her, he was so angry and sad that tears came to his eyes. Suddenly he saw a turtle creeping slowly toward him. In the afternoon sunlight the tortoise shell on its back gleamed like gold. As it came nearer, the young man rubbed his eyes in astonishment, for the turtle really was gold and, more than that, when it got near him, it opened its golden mouth and asked what was troubling him.

The young man gasped in amazement. This must be the idol, Kim Qui, the very one who had appeared to the Emperor An Duong Vuong centuries ago and told him how to defeat the Chinese. Perhaps Kim Qui would help him also. So the young man told the idol the whole story and how his wife had stolen the magic jade and run away.

"I will help you," said Kim Qui. "Here are two flowers, one red and one white. Go to the home of your wife's family and fasten this white flower on to their garden gate. Watch carefully, for something strange will happen and only this red flower will cure them." With that, the idol disappeared.

The young man did what the idol told him to do, and after he had fastened the white flower to the garden gate he hid himself in some tall bamboo to watch what would happen.

The fragrance of the white flower filled the air and seemed to grow stronger and stronger. Soon everyone in the house came out to see what flower was making the sweet perfume. When they saw the strange flower on the garden gate they picked it off and passed it from one to another to inhale its fragrance. Immediately their noses began to grow. They grew and grew until they were as long as elephant trunks. The people had to hold them up to keep them from dragging on the ground.

What a sight they were, to be sure. Soon their screams and groans brought all the people in the village to see what was the matter. The wise men tried every remedy they could think of, but nothing made the noses any shorter. "What a strange disease," they said. "It must be some great punishment for an evil deed. What could it be?"

"I will tell you," said the young man, stepping from the clump of bamboo. "My wife stole my magic jade and returned home to live with her family. If they will give me back my jade, I will promise to shorten their noses."

Quickly they gave him his jade and he gave them the red flower to smell, and soon their noses were as short as ever. The wife very meekly followed her husband back to his home and from that time on they lived happily together.

The Princess of
Mount Nam-Nhu

The old monk leaned on his rake and looked proudly around the temple garden. Never had it looked more beautiful. Every flower bed was a mass of bloom and every blossom was perfect. Not a weed, not a beetle spoiled the picture. Even the gravel in the paths had been raked into patterns of long sweeping curves. As he picked up a twig that had just fallen, the old monk thought what a perfect day it was for the Flower Festival. Soon all the villagers and strangers from far away would be strolling through this garden to enjoy its beauty and to reflect on the wonders of nature. Tu Thuc, the mandarin's son, would be there. Even now he was in the temple attending the early morning service.

From the pagoda came the chanting of the monks and the aromatic fragrance of incense. Soon the big bronze bell would sound and the morning service would be over. The old monk gave one last sweep with his rake, picked up one blossom that had fallen from the flowering peach tree, and hurried away to his cottage behind the garden wall.

As the bells rang out, the doors of the pagoda were thrown open and the villagers came down the steps and into the garden. First came the mandarin's son, Tu Thuc, a handsome young man wearing a scarlet silk coat heavy with gold embroidery. His face beamed with pleasure and his eyes sparkled with anticipation. He loved all growing things and, it was rumored, neglected his duties at his father's court in order to roam across the fields of his father's farms, watching the peasants planting or harvesting rice. Here in the temple garden he could feast his eyes on beauty, and the pleasure he took in wandering leisurely down the paths could be seen in the way he lingered over an especially beautiful blossom to inhale its fragrance or to tenderly touch a single petal.

Following him came the villagers, dressed in their best and walking sedately. This was a day they loved. In all the province of Tien Du there was no garden equal to this one, and today they were allowed to wander freely through it as long as they wished.

Unnoticed by the villagers, a beautiful girl in a dress of strange design stood hesitantly on the steps of the pagoda and looked in amazement at the masses of flowers and the fruit trees in blossom. Slowly she walked to the first flower bed and gently touched a blossom. She stared curiously at every petal and leaf and leaned over to catch the fragrance as though she had never seen a flower before. She walked excitedly up one path and down another until at last she came to the flowering peach tree. Suddenly she broke off a small branch and started to run out of the garden.

At that moment the old monk returned and, seeing what she had done, called out, "Stop her! Stop her! She has broken a branch of the flowering peach tree!"

The villagers were stunned. How could anyone wish to destroy a single flower in this beautiful garden, much less break off a branch from the peach tree? Quickly they surrounded the strange girl until the monk could get to her.

At the far end of the garden Tu Thuc heard the angry cries and hurried to the pagoda to see what was the matter. He arrived in time to see the old monk lead the girl up the steps of the pagoda and through the open doors. Tu Thuc followed them and, once inside the temple, watched quietly as she was

being questioned by the monks. He wondered where she was from. Certainly not from his father's court nor from the villages nearby as she was not wearing the wide trousers and long overdress of Tien Du, but a long blue robe patterned with a design of white clouds. She was dressed as a lady of quality, but when the monks demanded payment for the damage she had done, she claimed she had no money.

Far from being defiant or proud, she seemed completely bewildered by the confusion, and when Tu Thuc saw the troubled look in her black eyes and the droop in her slender shoulders, he took pity on her and offered his own mandarin's coat to the monks if they would let the girl go free.

This they agreed to do and immediately helped him off with his splendid coat. Then he turned to speak to the girl and found to his amazement that she had disappeared. No one in the temple or the garden had seen her leave and although Tu Thuc ran out to the busy street and looked up and down, he could not see a sign of her.

For days the villagers talked of nothing but the stranger who had broken the branch of the flowering peach tree and had then disappeared. Where had she come from? Why had she done it? Where had she gone? At the court of the man-

darin, Tu Thuc found his thoughts continually straying to the beautiful girl in the strange blue robe. Each time he opened a book her sad, bewildered eyes stared back at him. Each time he went to the village he hoped to see her in the crowds.

At last he decided to leave his father's court and spend all of his time looking for her. He renounced his title, packed up what few things he wanted to take with him, and set out on his journey. For months he walked from village to village, hoping to find some trace of the girl, but no one had seen her.

Finally, at the end of a particularly hot, dusty journey, he
came to the seaside town of Than Phu. The road ran past a
small cove where emerald green waves washed up on a curve
of sandy beach. The water looked cool and inviting, so Tu
Thuc decided to refresh himself before going on into the town.
He stripped off his clothes and plunged in, swimming vigor-
ously for awhile, and then rolled over on his back to float
lazily in the cool blue water.

Overhead white birds circled against the sapphire sky and
billowy white clouds drifted slowly by. Far out to sea the
waves broke in a tumble of froth and foam on a sunken reef.
On one side of the cove rose tall cliffs with many crevices and
ledges. Tu Thuc scanned them carefully to see if he could see
any birds' nests, and as he did so he noticed high on one ledge
the opening to a cave.

Being a naturally curious person, Tu Thuc swam back to
shore, scrambled into his clothes and started to climb up the
steep sides of the cliff. When he got to the highest ledge he
found that the entrance to the cave was big enough to walk
into and the cave itself seemed to stretch far back under the
hill. The walls of the cave were streaked with curious colors
and all around were strange formations of rocks. In all his

long journey, Tu Thuc had never seen anything to equal it. On and on he walked, through long corridors of stone, marveling at everything he saw. Before he realized it, the light, which had been getting dimmer and dimmer, faded completely and Tu Thuc could only feel with his hands the walls beside him.

He turned to make his way back to the entrance, expecting to be guided by the bright sunshine outside, but alas, not a glimmer of light could he see. His eyes strained to see through the darkness, but even his hands in front of him were invisible. He felt his way, inch by inch, in what he hoped was the right direction. He groped his way slowly, feeling the walls with his hands and sliding one foot forward along the floor, for fear of falling into one of the deep holes he had seen on his way in.

At last, far ahead of him, he saw a faint light. He hurried as fast as he dared toward the opening, expecting to find the entrance in the cliff where he had come in, but when he got there he found the hole was just barely big enough to crawl through and once outside, instead of looking down on the green waters of the little cove, he saw nothing but a rolling mass of white clouds. As far as he could see, the clouds stretched like a snowy countryside with hills and valleys and here and there a high billowy tower. A strange light, not like sunlight, came from somewhere, tinting the clouds rose and gold and shading the valleys with mauve. In the middle of this field of clouds rose the highest mountain Tu Thuc had ever seen. Its sides were purple in the strange light, and on the lower peaks were built beautiful castles. The castles were pale green or white and gleamed softly, like precious jade.

Tu Thuc was speechless with wonder. He could do nothing but stare in admiration at the scene before him. Gradually he became aware of singing around him and then soft, gay laughter. Turning his head, he saw two blue-robed girls walking toward him across the white clouds.

When they got near him the taller one said, "Oh, our bridegroom has come." Then they both bowed respectfully to him and said, "We are sorry that we are late. Our Lady is waiting for you. Please come with us." At that, they each took him by the hand and started to lead him across the field of clouds toward one of the jade castles.

At first he stumbled and staggered as he tried to walk on the soft clouds, but soon he felt lighter and found that his footsteps were getting longer, as though he were almost flying. In no time at all they reached the castle and the two

young girls led him into a spacious room whose walls of jade
were carved with designs of flowers and birds. At one end of
the room was a dais and on it a couch made of mother-of-pearl.
Reclining on the couch was a beautiful woman who summoned Tu Thuc to her.

Motioning for him to sit on a large silvery cushion by her
couch, she said, "Tu Thuc, you have been traveling far and
wide for many months. Do you know where you are now?"

Tu Thuc shook his head. "To tell you the truth," he said,
"I don't recognize a thing. I have seen many strange sights
and visited many strange places, but never have I seen so
beautiful a place as this. Would you mind telling me where
this is?"

"It is not surprising that you don't know where you are,"
said the lady, smiling at him. "You have come through one
of the thirty-six caves in the mountain called Phu-Lai and
have walked across the Path of the Clouds to the mountain
you are now on, Mount Nam-Nhu. Far beneath you, under
the clouds, lies the ocean. The foothills of our mountain do not
reach the sea; they disappear in the clouds and the mountain
floats over the sea. I am the Lady of Mount Nam-Nhu."

Then the lady motioned for the two girls to open a hidden

door in the jade walls and out stepped a beautiful young girl, with downcast eyes. Shyly she came forward and stood before the dais. One look at her face told Tu Thuc that she was the girl for whom he had been searching. He started to speak to her, but the lady interrupted. "This is my daughter, Giang Huong, who once broke a branch of flowering peach tree in the garden of the pagoda at Tien Du. Here in fairyland we do not have flowering peach trees and Giang Huong wished us to see the beautiful blossoms. She meant no harm, but she should not have touched them. It was no wonder the monks were angry. I have not forgotten how you saved her. As a reward for your kindness I offer you her hand in marriage and hope that you will accept it and will stay here and live with us."

Tu Thuc agreed, and the marriage was celebrated that very day. All the fairies of the land came to wish the young couple happiness and the Lady of Mount Nam-Nhu rejoiced that her daughter had found such a fine husband.

Time passed pleasantly for Tu Thuc. With his beautiful bride at his side, he explored every ridge and valley of Phu-Lai. Each day brought some new pleasure, and life for him would have continued as an endless honeymoon if, once through a rift in the clouds, he had not caught sight of the ocean. Far below him he could see the dark blue of the deep water and a tiny boat being rowed to shore.

From then on, Tu Thuc yearned to return to his own land. He remembered the sights and sounds of the peasants working on his father's farms and the smells of the village market place. He remembered how grieved his father had been when he had renounced his title, and how his mother had wept when he had left his home. The more he brooded over these things the more he wanted to see his own land and his own people once more. He became moody and silent and withdrawn.

When Giang Huong found out what was troubling him she said, "For a year we have lived happily together. I cannot believe that you are still thinking of your own world. Why would you want to return to earth where life is so short? However, you must do as you wish. Only remember that if you leave, we may never see each other again."

Much as he loved Giang Huong, the desire to return to his own country and to see his mother and father again grew stronger and stronger. Sadly he told his wife that he wished to return to earth. She gave him a carriage drawn by two white swans and a fairy to lead him through the cave and, weeping bitterly, bade him farewell.

In just a few minutes Tu Thuc was once more at the entrance of the cave where his adventures had started a year ago. He looked down at the little cove and the waves washing up on the beach. As he climbed down the cliff he was surprised to find several small shrubs growing in the crevices and marveled at how quickly they had grown in one year. Once safely down on the beach, it seemed to him that the trees were much taller than he remembered them.

It took him some time to make his way back to his own village, as many new roads had been built and he had to stop frequently to ask his way. Even his father's farms had changed, with new buildings and new dikes around the rice fields. The small market place of the village was now three times its size and busy streets led from it in all directions. The pagoda with its gardens was completely surrounded with stores and offices and there was nothing left of the flowering peach tree except a gnarled stump. Try as he might, Tu Thuc could not even find his own home, and when he asked the way people shook their heads and hurried on. Some even looked at him as though they thought he was mad.

Finally a gray-bearded elder tapped him on the shoulder and said, "When I was a child my grandfather told me about a mandarin's son who had the same name as yours. He left home years and years ago and met with a great misfortune, for he was buried in a cave in the cliffs of Than Phu."

With this, Tu Thuc realized that a year in fairyland was equal to one hundred years on earth and that his long journey back to his home was fruitless. He thought longingly of his beautiful wife and, with an aching heart, started back on the road to Than Phu.

A fisherman claims he saw Tu Thuc climb up the face of the cliff and walk through the entrance of the cave, and that he heard the sound of soft, gay laughter as Tu Thuc disappeared from sight. And from that day to this no one ever saw him again. Some think the fairies were waiting for him to guide him through the cave so that he could return to Giang Huong and be with her forever.

Why the Monsoon Comes
Each Year

The Princess Mi Nuong was sad. She sat quietly with down-cast eyes while a handmaiden combed her glossy, black hair and idly smoothed a fold in the silk of her gown. When the last jade pin was fastened in her hair and the handmaiden held up a mirror, she pushed it away without even glancing in it. She already knew what the mirror would show her: a tiny new wrinkle between her eyes. It was this new wrinkle that made her sad. She was growing old and she was hus-bandless.

It wasn't that she was ugly or lame or bad tempered. She had had many suitors. Some were handsome and many had come from foreign lands, but not one had gained the consent of her father, the Emperor. Like many fathers with only one

child, he believed that no one was good enough for his charming daughter. For her he wanted someone rich and distinguished and, above all, powerful. Years had passed since the last suitor had proposed and been declined, and it looked as though the Princess would remain single forever.

Then one day two strangers appeared at the Emperor's

court. Both were very handsome, both were very rich, and one was the powerful Spirit of the Sea and the other was the equally powerful Spirit of the Mountain. Since both suitors arrived at exactly the same time, and met with equal favor in the eyes of the Emperor, he was hard put to choose between them. So he told them that whoever first brought his betrothal gifts the next day would have the hand of the Princess and could leave with her immediately.

The Spirit of the Sea rushed back to the ocean and summoned his men. He commanded them to search for the most perfect pearls, the tastiest crabs, and the juiciest squid. The Spirit of the Mountain climbed to the highest peak and gathered his men about him. Then he opened his magic book and wished for the gifts he wanted to present to the Princess. He wished for his men to find a chest of diamonds and emeralds that had been hidden in a dark cave in the mountains for hundreds of years, and he wished for them to fill baskets with rare fruits that couldn't be grown at the Emperor's court.

Presently the men appeared before the Spirit of the Mountain with the casket of jewels and baskets of strawberries, peaches, and grapes. Then, while the Spirit of the Sea was still searching the depths of the ocean for his gifts, the Spirit of the Mountain with his men was on his way down the mountainside to be first at the gates of the Emperor's palace. He arrived there just as dawn was breaking, and claimed Mi Nuong as his bride. The Emperor was delighted with the gifts of jewels and fruit, and felt that surely he had made a good match for his daughter. He sent her off with the Spirit of the Mountain and promised to visit her in her new home as soon as she was settled.

Mi Nuong and her husband were barely outside the gates of the Emperor's palace when along the road from the sea came the Spirit of the Sea with his men bearing great trays of pearls and dishes of delicious sea food. When the Spirit of the Sea saw that he was late by just a few minutes and that the sun was barely over the horizon, he was very angry. He suspected that the Spirit of the Mountain had used some tricks to get there first and so he commanded his followers to pursue the Spirit of the Mountain and take Mi Nuong away from him.

With that, the wind began to blow and the rain fell and the ocean rose higher and higher. Soon foaming waves were breaking over the land, and the people had to flee for their lives. All of the creatures of the sea turned into soldiers of

the Spirit of the Sea and ran screaming up the road to over-
take the Spirit of the Mountain before he could get to the high
ground where he ruled. Wherever they passed, the rivers rose
into floods, houses were washed away, and whole cities were
left in ruins. The water rose higher and higher, until waves
were breaking at the foot of the mountain, but still the Spirit
of the Sea had not caught up with Mi Nuong. Now the Spirit
of the Mountain ordered his men to throw huge logs and
boulders down on the Spirit of the Sea and his forces.

The battle between the two most powerful spirits continued
both day and night, and the poor people of the villages prayed
for them to stop. Many had been drowned in the flood; some
had been struck by lightning. Their crops had been washed
away, as well as their homes. Finally, the Spirit of the Mountain used his magic wishing book to wish his mountain to
grow higher. Then he took Mi Nuong and his men to the
very highest peak, well out of reach of the Spirit of the Sea.

When the Spirit of the Sea saw that his attempt to overcome the Spirit of the Mountain was in vain, he retreated with
his soldiers back to the ocean, taking the flood waters with
him. But so angry was he at his defeat that every year he tries
again to defeat the Spirit of the Mountain and win the Prin-

cess Mi Nuong to be his own wife. Every year he sends storms and floods up the river valleys to the very foot of the mountain where Mi Nuong still lives with her husband. And each year he is again defeated and forced to withdraw to his home in the ocean. And that is why the monsoon comes each year in Viet Nam.

The Emperor's
Magic Bow

Long, long ago in a time that is hard to remember, when
Viet Nam was called Au Lac, the people were peaceful farmers. All they wanted was to be free to plant and harvest their
rice and melons, gather a few coconuts, and maybe catch a
fish or two, and live a pleasant, quiet life. But north of Au Lac
lived the Chinese who were eager to get more land for themselves. Time and time again they sent down armies to try to
defeat the people in Au Lac and take their land away from
them.

Finally the Emperor An Duong Vuong decided to build a
great wall just north of the city of Co Loa to separate Au Lac
from China. Such a wall would be easy to defend and would
keep the armies in the north from invading his country.

Thousands of peasants worked for months to carry out the Emperor's orders, but everything seemed against them. In the hot sun the mud cracked and the stones worked loose, falling down and killing many workers. Each time the wall was half-way up it crumbled like dried clay and fell in ruins. Soon the peasants began to think there were evil spirits working against them, and they became so frightened they ran away to their homes. Work on the wall came to a stop.

The Emperor An Duong Vuong called a meeting of his bravest generals. As he waited for them to arrive he paced the floor and read for the third time the message that had just been delivered to him. "Imperial Majesty," it said, "the Co Loa wall has fallen again. We do not know the cause. Three times we have built it at your Majesty's command, and three times it has collapsed before we could finish it. Some evil spirit does not wish this wall to stand between Au Lac and China."

When the Emperor read the message to his generals, they shook their heads in bewilderment.

"Is it possible to defend Au Lac from our enemies, the Chinese, without this wall?" asked the Emperor.

The generals considered for a moment and then replied,

"Without the Co Loa wall we will be vanquished in a month. Already the Chinese troops are marching toward us. A way must be found to make the wall stand. Let us go to the pagoda and pray for help."

That night, after all the generals had left, An Duong Vuong knelt in the privacy of his bedchamber and prayed for help. Suddenly there appeared before him a golden turtle. It was the idol, Kim Qui, that had left its temple and was standing before him. As the Emperor stared in surprise at his unusual visitor, the golden turtle began to speak. It told the

Emperor just how to build the Co Loa wall so that it would stand, and how to defend it when it was under attack. Then it took from one golden claw a curved golden nail and told the Emperor to build a new bow, using the golden nail at the tip. If he did this the bow would have magic powers and with it he could defeat his enemies and destroy the evil spirits that had been working against him.

The Emperor followed the idol's advice and the Co Loa wall was built without delay. He also had built the bow, using the golden nail from the golden turtle's claw at the tip. When the Chinese attacked from the north, the Emperor used his magic bow and defeated the troops each time they advanced. The magic bow was as powerful as Kim Qui said it would be. Soon the enemies of Au Lac were vanquished and the Emperor An Duong Vuong ruled happily over his people.

Now the Chinese General, Trieu Da, whose soldiers had been defeated in battle, was very angry and decided to try another way to conquer Au Lac. He ordered his son, Trong Thuy, to journey to Au Lac, make peace with the Emperor and marry the Emperor's daughter, the beautiful My Chau, thereby uniting the two countries through marriage.

Trong Thuy did as his father commanded, and since he

was a handsome, intelligent young man with a gift for diplomacy, it soon came to pass that peace was declared between the two countries and Trong Thuy won My Chau as his bride.

One evening, shortly after they were married, as the young

couple strolled in the garden, Trong Thuy asked My Chau why it was the Chinese forces had been defeated every time they had attacked the Co Loa wall. Now My Chau had been brought up, as all proper Vietnamese girls are, to be obedient to her husband, and so without any hesitation, she told him about the magic bow and how the idol Kim Qui had advised her father on how to build the wall.

From that time on, every moment Trong Thuy had alone he spent it building a bow that looked exactly like the magic bow, and one day when the Emperor was holding court in the throne room, Trong Thuy stole into the Emperor's bed-chamber and took the magic bow, leaving in its place the bow he himself had made. Then he told the Emperor that he had received word that his father was sick and wished to see him, and asked permission of the Emperor to return to China for a short visit. Wishing to please his new son-in-law, and gain favor with his former enemy, An Duong Vuong readily gave his permission for the trip.

My Chau was heartbroken at the thought of being separated from her husband by even a few days and begged to go with him, but Trong Thuy told her the trip would be too tiring and that he could travel faster alone. As he took his leave he said, "My beloved, although there is peace between our two countries, Au Lac still has many enemies. If, by chance, war should break out while I am gone and you should have to flee from our home, how will I find you?"

"I have a goose-feather coat," replied My Chau. "If I have to leave, I will wear it and drop goose feathers along the way. Then you have merely to follow the goose feathers to find me."

When Trong Thuy arrived in China, he hurried to the home of his father, Trieu Da, to give him the magic bow and tell him all that he had learned about the building of the Co Loa wall. The General was very pleased with what his son reported to him and rejoiced that he had been able to steal the magic bow. A great banquet was prepared to celebrate his home-coming and fireworks brightened the sky the whole night long.

The next day General Trieu Da ordered his Chinese troops to march on Au Lac and attack the Co Loa wall again. With the magic bow in his own hands, he knew his soldiers would be victorious. As soon as word reached Emperor An Duong Vuong that the Chinese army was approaching, he reached for his magic bow and, not seeing that it was the false one, mounted his horse and galloped as fast as he could to the Co Loa wall. Once there, he took a position where he could shoot at the advancing troops of the Chinese but not get hit himself. Arrow after arrow he shot at the troops, but not one soldier did he hit. Each arrow fell short of its mark and broke into splinters on the ground. He tried raising his aim and tried using arrows of different lengths, but to no avail. There was something wrong with the bow; it had lost its magic.

By this time the Chinese were close to the wall and the Emperor, afraid of being captured, leaped on his horse and raced back to his palace. There he found his daughter, My Chau, and pulled her up into the saddle behind him and galloped away to the South.

After a day of hard riding they came to the foot of a mountain. Here the road ended, and there was no way around the mountain. The sea was on one side and the jungle on the other. To climb up the steep sides of the mountain was impossible. The Emperor was in despair and, without realizing it, cried aloud, "Kim Qui, Kim Qui, is it here that you wish me to die?"

At that moment the golden turtle walked across the road.

"Your Majesty," said the idol, "you have left the Chinese far behind you. You are safe from capture. Your ancient enemy is not the one to fear. Your real enemy sits behind you." And with that the idol vanished.

An Duong Vuong turned his head and saw his daughter sitting in the saddle behind him wearing her goose-feather coat. Most of the feathers were gone now, as she had been scattering them along the trail. Then the Emperor realized that it was she who had betrayed him. He drew his sword and with one blow cut off her head. Then he threw himself into the sea and was never seen again.

In the meantime, Trong Thuy had followed the Chinese troops over the Co Loa wall and into Au Lac and, remembering his wife's promise, looked for the trail of goose feathers. At the palace steps he found it and followed it south until he, too, came to the end of the road at the foot of the mountain. There he found the body of his wife. At last he realized what he had done. He had sacrificed his beautiful wife for the selfish ambitions of his father. Tears streamed down his cheeks as he wrapped her in his own cloak and laid her to rest in a grave by the sea. And then, overcome by grief and shame, he leaped from the highest cliff and was dashed to death on the rocks below.

The Farmer, the Buffalo, and the Tiger

One day a farmer was plowing a field with his water buffalo. They had been working hard since early dawn, and by noon both man and beast were hot and tired and hungry. However, the farmer didn't want to stop until he had finished plowing the field, so he picked up a stick and began beating the buffalo to make him walk faster. Every time the buffalo stumbled or stopped to rest, the farmer would shout at him and whack him with the stick until the poor animal was ready to drop with fatigue. So intent was the farmer on getting his work done, he didn't notice that a large, yellow tiger had appeared at the edge of the field and was sitting in the shade of the trees watching what was going on.

Finally the field was finished and the farmer untied the

buffalo from the plow and led him to a nearby field and turned him loose to graze. Then the farmer walked across the field to his little hut to have his own meal of tea and rice. When he was out of sight, the tiger strolled over to the buffalo, looked pityingly at him and said, "My poor, foolish buffalo, what a coward you are! Why do you work so hard for the farmer? Why do you let him beat you and then, at the end of your day's work, let him turn you into this parched field to hunt for your own food? Why don't you fight him? With your size and sharp horns, you could beat him easily. Then you would be free to live at liberty as I do."

"You are the king of all the animals," said the buffalo, "and have lived all your life in the jungle. You have never lived with man and so do not know him well. Although he looks small and weak, he is the real king of all creatures, including you."

"How can that be?" answered the tiger angrily. "How can they be so powerful when they can't do the things we do? They have no wings to fly like birds, they can't run as fast as deer, and their teeth aren't as sharp as mine. To me they seem very weak."

"Yes, I know they are small and weak, but their intelligence

is greater than anything under the sun," replied the buffalo.

"I don't believe it," said the tiger. "When your master comes back, just show me this intelligence of his."

When the farmer returned to the field he was startled to see a tiger talking to his buffalo and wished he had some weapon for protection. However, the buffalo assured his master that the tiger meant no harm and only wanted to ask him some questions.

"I have heard about your intelligence," said the tiger. "I understand that it is greater than anything under the sun. Where do you keep it? Would you mind letting me see it?"

"I would be very glad to show you my intelligence, but since I keep it in a bag at home, I can't show it to you now," replied the farmer as he started leading his buffalo toward home.

"Don't go away. Please come back," said the tiger.

"You are very cunning, but you can't deceive me," said the farmer. "If I come back you will kill my buffalo and eat him."

"I swear I won't kill him. In fact, I'll protect him from every danger while you are gone. Do let me see your intelligence, please," replied the tiger.

"You can swear all you like," said the farmer, "but I will only show you my intelligence if you will let me tie you up until I get back."

"All right," said the tiger. "If this intelligence is so good, I want to see it."

With that, the farmer took a rope off his plow and tied the tiger tightly to a tree. Then he picked up his plow and beat the tiger over the head until he was dead. Seeing how well the man had outwitted the tiger, the buffalo shook with glee. In fact, he laughed so hard he hit his teeth on a big rock, and that is why buffalo have no teeth now.

The Magic Ruby

Once upon a time there was a hunter named Khan who knew every animal in the forest and every bird and snake as well. One day as he was passing some rocks where he knew there was a family of black snakes, he saw the female black snake crawl out of her cave and into the cave of a white snake on the other side of the hill. Khan knew that the male black snake would be angry at such a betrayal, so he took his bow and arrow and shot at the female black snake who, by this time, was so interested in the white snake she had forgotten all about her own family in her own cave.

The female snake was alarmed to find herself pierced by Khan's arrow and tried to crawl back across the hill and into her own cave, but just as she got to it, she died. Soon her mate returned and when he found her lying dead in front of their cave, with an arrow with Khan's name on it, he was very angry and made a promise to his wife's soul to be revenged. That evening the black snake crawled into Khan's house and lay in wait for him on a big beam right over the place where Khan spread his sleeping mat.

It was very hot that night and Khan tossed and turned on his sleeping mat and finally got up and sat in the doorway of his hut to get what little breeze was blowing. His wife was restless, too, and came and sat beside him and they began to talk about the day's events. Khan told her how he had killed a female black snake who had gone to the cave of a white snake while her own mate was out getting food for her and her family.

When the black snake heard this he realized how his wife had betrayed him and that Khan was his true friend. He was ashamed of his anger and that he had sought vengeance. He slid along the beam and out through a hole in the thatched roof and crawled down the side of the hut to the ground in front of Khan. There he coiled himself up most politely and said, "My dear friend, you were right to kill my unfaithful wife and I thank you very much. In return, I shall give you a reward. Here is a stone, a magic stone, that will let you hear

and understand all the languages around you, even the languages of animals, and birds, and insects." With this he opened his mouth and out dropped a large ruby which Khan

picked up and carefully tied in a piece of cloth which he wound around his head.

From that time on, Khan could understand everything everyone said, even the animals, and he spent much of his time listening to the conversations of the birds and insects. One day when he was out hunting a raven flew by and said, "Khan, you need not hunt any more. Come to the edge of the forest and you will find a lame deer. You have merely to pick it up and take it home." Then, after a pause, the raven added, "And remember, Khan, after you have killed it, give me its heart."

Khan agreed, and followed the raven to the edge of the forest. He soon came to the place where a deer had fallen and broken its leg. Quickly he killed it and cleaned it and carried it home, but he forgot to give the heart to the raven. Soon the raven swooped down on Khan, beating him with its wings and pecking him with its beak and screaming insults and threats to him. Khan became so angry that he drew his bow and shot an arrow at the raven. The bird flew out of reach of the arrow and, instead of the arrow hitting him, he caught it in his claws and flew away with it, screaming, "Revenge, revenge!"

Some days later, a man was found killed by an arrow with Khan's name on it. Khan swore that he had not killed the man—in fact, had never seen him—but he could not explain how an arrow with his name on it had pierced the man's body. It never occurred to him that this was the way in which the raven was taking his revenge. Khan was brought into court and charged with murder, and since he couldn't explain about his arrow, he was taken off to prison and thrown into a narrow cell with nothing to sleep on except the bare ground and nobody to talk to except the jailer who brought him his meal of rice twice a day. All day long he had nothing to do but sit and think about the arrow and wonder how it had killed the stranger when he hadn't shot it.

Fortunately, he still had his magic ruby with him and could spend his time listening to the conversations of the ants that ran across the ground. There were two long lines of them coming and going through a crack in the wall of his cell. They were bringing in bits of food from the outside and storing it in a hole in a wooden post that supported the ceiling, and then returning for more. One day when the ants had been particularly busy he heard one ant say, "Hurry, hurry! We haven't much time. There's going to be a big flood and all the crops will be destroyed."

Another ant said, "It will be hard to find food. All the grain in the mandarin's storerooms has been destroyed by weevils."

When the jailer brought Khan his evening bowl of rice, Khan told him what he had heard from the ants. Instead of laughing at him, the jailer told the officer of the guard, who told it to the mandarin, whereupon the mandarin ordered an inspection to be made of his storerooms. His servants were amazed to find that all the grain had been destroyed by weevils, just as Khan had said. Shortly after this, the rain started to fall and continued for days and days until the rivers overflowed their banks and flooded the countryside for miles around and all the crops were destroyed. The mandarin was so impressed with Khan's ability to foretell the future that he asked to see him.

The jailer brought Khan to the throne room and the mandarin asked him how it was he could read the future. Khan told him the whole story, from the time he killed the snake, and showed the mandarin the ruby. After hearing the story, the mandarin set Khan free and found him work to do at court, but first made Khan give him the magic ruby.

With the magic ruby in his possession, the mandarin lost no time in listening to the talk of all the animals and birds and insects. In fact, he became so interested in this he had little time to attend to the affairs of state. It would have gone badly for the country if the mandarin hadn't lost the ruby, quite by accident. One day while he was traveling down the Mekong River by boat he dropped it overboard. He had been trying to listen to what the fish were saying and the ruby slipped through his fingers and sank through the water and out of sight. The mandarin was distressed that his own carelessness had lost him the magic ruby and spared no expense to try to recover it. He sent his best divers down to search the bottom of the river, but all they came up with were handfuls of mud. Finally, he called Khan to him and ordered him to look for it.

For years Khan searched for the ruby. He looked along every foot of the river bottom and followed it curve by curve all the way to the sea. There he fell sick and died, but since he had been so faithful to the task the mandarin had set for him, he was allowed to return in another form and go on living as a tiny, white crab.

And even today, if you go to the seashore, you may see him burrowing in the sand, patiently heaping up little piles of sand which the waves soon wash away, and digging hole after hole, still hunting for the magic ruby.

Three Who Couldn't
Be Parted

Long, long ago there were two brothers who looked so much alike that even their parents could not tell them apart. When they were grown to be young men, the elder fell in love with a girl from a nearby village and soon married her and brought her home to live. The younger brother was very unhappy at this state of affairs, as he also was in love with the girl and found it hard to see her around the house every day and know that she could never be his wife. However, out of loyalty to his elder brother, he made the best of it and the three spent many pleasant hours together.

One day while the two brothers were out hunting in the forest, the younger brother began to feel sick, so he took leave of his elder brother and hastened home alone. When he got there the girl mistook him for her husband and spoke loving words to him and caressed him and clung to him in such a way that the poor young man was afraid to stay in the house with her. So, sick as he was, he packed up his few possessions and left the house, for fear of dishonoring his brother's name.

When the elder brother came home and asked his wife how the younger brother was feeling, she realized the mistake she had made, and was ashamed at what she had done. She confessed to her husband that she had made love to his younger brother by mistake and begged his forgiveness. Knowing how much his younger brother looked like him, the elder brother forgave his wife and told her he would explain everything to his younger brother. The wife then told him that the younger brother had packed his things and had left the house. This worried the elder brother because he knew the young man was sick and, besides, it grieved him to think that his brother felt driven from his home. Quickly he packed up some food for a long journey and started out to find the younger brother.

Once he had gotten away from the house, the younger brother began to feel better, and since he couldn't turn around and go back, he decided he might as well set forth to see the

world. He walked and walked past all the villages he knew, through dense forests and across broad meadows, until at last he came to a big, deep river he had never seen before. The river was much too wide to swim across, and there was no bridge and the only trees that could be cut down to use as a bridge or a raft were too far away. By this time he was so tired that he sat down on the river bank to think things over and immediately he died and turned into a big limestone rock.

In the meantime, the elder brother was following all the paths through the forests that he and his brother used in hunting. He looked for his younger brother everywhere and, finally, after many days of walking, he too came to the big, deep river. He tried and tried to find some way to get across it, as he was sure his younger brother must be on the other side. At last he gave up and sat down on the limestone rock to rest a minute, and the very second he sat on the rock he died and turned into an areca tree.

Back home, the young wife waited and waited for the two brothers to return. She was grief-sticken, because she felt that everything was her fault. Days went by, and weeks, and still the men had not returned. Finally she decided to go look for both of them. She followed their trail through the forests and across meadows until at last she came to the same river that had stopped the brothers. By this time she was too tired to even think about finding a way across, but sat down on the limestone rock to rest and immediately she died and turned into a betel plant.

As years went by, the areca tree grew taller and taller and the betal plant soon covered the rock and started to climb up the areca tree. The roots of the areca tree spread and crept into every little crevice of the limestone rock until the natives couldn't tell where one started and the other began. And it was then that they got the idea of combining the areca nut, the betel leaf, and powdered limestone to make a pleasant tidbit to chew on. In the mountain regions of Viet Nam the natives still chew this combination and think it helps to preserve their teeth.

The Author

Dorothy Lewis Robertson was born in New York City, received a B.S. degree in speech and English from Columbia University, and an M.A. in dramatic arts from the University of North Carolina. She has been an instructor in speech and dramatics at American University and Smith College, and is currently active in community theatre and creative dramatics for children in Orient, New York, where she now lives.

Boating, hiking, and gardening occupy leisure hours for Mrs. Robertson and her husband. She also is a storyteller at the library in Greenport where these Vietnamese tales have found an enthusiastic audience.

The Illustrator

Born in Poland, W. T. Mars was graduated from the Academy of Fine Arts in Warsaw and later studied in France, Germany, and Italy. His paintings have been exhibited in London, Glasgow, and Edinburgh, among other places. His first illustrations were done as a child for a story written by his mother, a well-known author of children's books.

Mr. Mars lived in London after World War II and came to the United States in 1952. He has illustrated numerous volumes in the children's field, including his own first book, THE BABY DRAGON. He and his wife live in New York on Long Island.